Simon
Aliens

Eva Mills
Illustrated by Gus Gordon

A Haights Cross Communications Company

Published by
Sundance Publishing
234 Taylor Street
Littleton, MA 01460

Copyright © text Eva Mills
Copyright © illustrations Gus Gordon
Project commissioned and managed by
Lorraine Bambrough-Kelly, The Writer's Style
Designed by Cath Lindsey/design rescue

First published 1998 by
Addison Wesley Longman Australia Pty Limited
95 Coventry Street
South Melbourne 3205 Australia
Exclusive United States Distribution: Sundance Publishing

ISBN 0-7608-3293-5

CONTENTS

For Simon

CHAPTER 1

Yap and Simon on the Paper Route

Simon threw the last newspaper as hard as he could toward Mrs. McGillicuddy's front door. *Thump!* The satisfying sound of the rolled-up paper hitting the front door brought a smile to Simon's face.

"Yap, yap, yap!" Simon's little terrier wasn't satisfied. She raced for the paper, picked it up in her mouth, and charged back to Simon.

"No, no, no!" scolded Simon, as he reached down to take the paper. "You're only supposed to bring it back if I miss, Yap." The terrier wagged her tail excitedly.

"I guess you'll never win any awards for intelligence, Yap," said Simon, "but you're still my favorite assistant paper-deliverer. We make a good team, don't we?"

"Yap!"

Simon reached down to give her a pat before they set off for home.

"Last one home is an alien's breakfast!" called Simon, as he flew down the Studley Street hill, with Yap racing behind him.

The night air was cold as it rushed past Simon's face. For the thousandth time that week, he wished it were summer again, so he could do his paper route while it was still light.

They rounded the corner at the bottom of the street. Yap took off across the park like a mad thing, barking and barking at something up in the trees. Simon skidded his bike around and stopped at the edge of the park.

"Yap!" he called. "Come here, you crazy dog! Stop barking at squirrels!"

Then Simon saw what Yap was barking at.
It wasn't in the trees—it was in the sky!
A bright, white light, about the size of a
streetlight, but much more powerful,
seemed to be floating above the park.

It was too bright to look directly at it for long. The light was beaming down on Yap, who had stopped barking. She just sat there looking up at it and wagging her tail.

Simon felt a shiver run up and down his spine. He knew it was a UFO.

Simon was scared, but he didn't want anything to happen to Yap. He ran into the park, entered the beam of light, and scooped her up. The light focused on him for a moment, and then it disappeared above the trees.

Simon's heart was beating fast. Holding Yap in his arms, he pedaled as fast as he could for home.

CHAPTER 2

UFO

"I'm sure it wasn't a UFO," said Simon's dad, "or else we would have seen it on the news."

"I'm sure it wasn't a UFO," said Simon's sister Becky, "or else there'd be aliens running up and down the street, blasting their way into people's houses and turning us into atomic particles."

"I *know* it wasn't a UFO," said Simon's mom. "It was the police helicopter. I saw it earlier, with its big searchlight beaming down into the park."

Simon didn't say anything.

The next night Simon saw the bright light again. He had just thrown Mr. Houey's paper straight into the fishpond. Yap was barking and barking at the slowly sinking newspaper.

"Vanishing Venusians!" muttered Simon under his breath. He took another newspaper up to the door, then retrieved Yap and the sopping-wet newspaper from the fishpond.

Just as Simon jumped back on his bike, the light appeared again overhead, hovering. Simon tried to convince himself it was just the police helicopter.

At the big old house with the overgrown yard, Simon threw the paper as far as he could up the long path. Yap squeezed through a gap in the wire fence and raced after the newspaper. The bright light still hovered overhead.

"Take it to the front door, Yap!" called Simon.

But Yap had lost interest in sniffing the newspaper, and was scrambling around in some nearby bushes. The beam of light, which had followed Yap up the path, was now following her closely as she sniffed her way back to the newspaper.

SNIFF
SNIFF

The front door of the old house opened. As soon as Mr. Charles came down the steps to collect his paper, the bright light disappeared. It didn't move away or fade into the sky. It just suddenly wasn't there, as if it had been turned off.

Mr. Charles waved to Simon and gave Yap a pat before going inside with his paper.

As soon as Mr. Charles went back inside his house, the light reappeared. It followed Yap as she trotted back to Simon.

Simon began to feel very uneasy. The sooner he finished his paper route, the better.

As they rounded the corner onto Hedge Street, the Hubers' dog, Cuddles, started barking and growling and snarling and snapping.

Cuddles was *big* and *tough* and *mean*. He made sure all the other dogs, and all the paper carriers, too, knew that he ruled the neighborhood.

Yap started barking back at Cuddles as she raced along the sidewalk toward the Hubers' house. The bright light followed her.

Simon's uneasiness shifted to fear. He pushed down hard on his brakes. "Wait, Yap!" he called. "Come back here!"

But Yap was too busy teasing Cuddles, jumping up and down on one side of the high picket fence. Cuddles was on the other side, growling and whining and trying to get his teeth through the gaps in the fence to reach Yap.

Now the bright light hovered above both dogs. The light grew stronger and brighter, until the whole street was as bright as day. The two dogs stopped snapping and snarling and barking, and they looked up into the light, wagging their tails!

As the light moved lower and lower, Simon could see that it was coming from an enormous alien spacecraft that looked a little like Yap's plastic bone.

Now, the spacecraft was at treetop level.
A high-pitched whistling noise came from
it. The light still shone on two dogs, who
were still wagging their tails and looking up
at the light.

Simon felt sick. He knew that if he didn't take Yap away right now, something awful was going to happen—but he was too late.

A high-pitched squeal came from the spacecraft, and Yap and Cuddles disappeared, transported up by the beam of light.

"No!" screamed Simon as he dropped his bike and threw himself into the beam of light. "Give me back my dog!" he yelled.

There was no response. The light was no longer painful to look at, but had become soft and almost friendly.

Then the high-pitched whistling began again. The light became brighter and brighter. There was one final squeal and *shwoop*. And then Simon, too, was sucked up by the beam of light, right into the alien spacecraft.

CHAPTER 3

Aboard the Spacecraft

Simon looked around. He was sitting on a raised platform with a number of padded chairs of various shapes and sizes. "This must be a transport area," he thought, standing up slowly.

He was obviously in the main control room of the spacecraft. The walls were filled with screens, dials, buttons, and flashing lights. The ceiling was covered with pipes and ducts of all shapes and sizes.

Below the platform was a long and narrow room. Aliens moved about busily.

"Hey!" he called out, but no one heard him.

They were all crowded in one corner of the room, peering at something.

Simon climbed down from the platform and walked over to see what all the fuss was about. There were Yap and Cuddles, sitting on a red velvet couch, being fed bits of meat from a silver platter!

"Yap!" he called, as he rushed forward.

The alien crowd gasped in horror. Two uniformed guards carrying scary-looking blasters rushed forward to block his way.

"You must not disturb the honored guests while they are eating," explained an important-looking alien in a blue robe.

munch munch
munch

"But . . . but . . . ," stammered Simon, "that's my pet dog!"

The crowd gasped again, and the blue-robed alien took Simon to one side. "Never use those words again!" he said severely. "We are from the Sirius Dog Star System. On our planet, Fidospot, the dogs are masters, and we are their loyal friends."

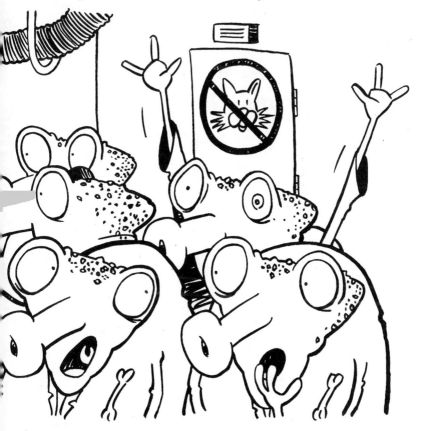

Yap saw Simon, and the terrier began barking frantically. She was trying to jump off the red velvet couch, but some unseen force held her to that spot.

Cuddles was munching away at the delicious food, his tail wagging happily. He looked up briefly to growl at Simon before returning to his meal.

Yap began whining and pawing at the couch.

"No, no, no!" wailed Simon. "You've got it all wrong! Yap's *my* loyal friend, and I'm *her* master!"

All of the aliens were now looking at Simon in horror.

The blue-robed alien was losing patience. "I must ask you to respect our intergalactic mission. Our masters have sent spacecraft to the four corners of the Solar System to see if there is intelligent life on any other planets. Finally, we have found it on your planet," he said, pointing to Yap and Cuddles.

"Intelligent life?" repeated Simon. "That's a joke!"

"That's enough!" the alien said angrily. "We transported you to our spaceship, thinking that you were a favored loyal friend to one of our honored guests. But I can see that you are nothing but an enemy. Guards!"

CHAPTER 4

Home Again

The uniformed aliens with the blasters moved up behind Simon, one on each side. They grabbed him by the arms.

"Transport him back to Earth!" commanded the blue-robed alien.

When Yap saw what was happening to Simon, she started barking and whining and growling, throwing herself around on the red velvet couch. But she was still held in the couch's force field.

Cuddles growled at Yap, and tried to jump off the couch. Soon both dogs were barking and thrashing around, trying to escape.

"No!" screamed Simon, kicking the guards and trying to free his arms. "I want Yap! Give me back my dog!"

The guards held him fast, dragged him back to the transport area, and marched him up the stairs to the platform. They forced Simon into one of the padded chairs and strapped him in.

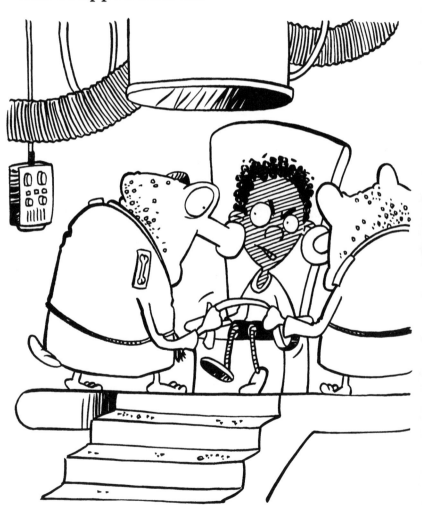

One of the guards pressed a big green button on the chair, and the bright light appeared all around them. As the guards stepped off the platform, the high-pitched whistling noise began. It became louder and louder.

"Yap!" yelled Simon. "Yap, over here!"

Yap and Cuddles were both thrashing around, trying to break the force that held them to the couch.

Suddenly, with a huge *bang,* the couch disappeared in a cloud of smoke. "Where are you, Yap? Over here!" Simon yelled.

The high-pitched whistling changed to a squeal, and a large door opened in the floor of the spacecraft. The transporting was about to begin.

Yap appeared out of the smoke, racing toward the transport platform. Just as Simon's skin began to tingle and the transport beam started to move him out of the chair, the little dog threw herself at the platform and jumped into his lap.

"Cuddles!" yelled Simon. "We can't go without Cuddles!"

A big, furry ball of dog hurled himself at the platform. Simon hauled Cuddles into the chair with Yap and him, just in time.

The three of them floated out of the spacecraft, and down the bright beam of light. They landed, *thump*, dumped on the street.

Simon woke up to the feel of Yap's tongue licking his face. "Urgh . . ." he groaned. "My head hurts!" He reached out to pat Yap, and the little dog licked him some more.

"Are you okay?"

Simon turned his head slowly. Mr. Huber was holding Cuddles by the collar and looking at him in a concerned way.

"Did you fall off your bike, Simon?"

"No . . ." said Simon, standing up carefully and looking around. His bike lay in a crumpled heap on the road. "That is . . . I don't know. Did you see anything odd, Mr. Huber?"

Mr. Huber shook his head. "I only came out because Cuddles was barking his head off. When I looked out the window, I saw him in the road. I don't know how he got out here . . . it's funny that he hasn't run away like he usually does when he gets out."

Simon picked up his bike and put all the newspapers back in the basket. Yap sat beside the bike, wagging her tail slowly and looking up at Simon.

"Are you sure you're okay?" asked
Mr. Huber, patting Cuddles, who was
whimpering and licking Mr. Huber's hand.

"Yeah, I'm fine," said Simon. "But I think I'll ask my sister Becky to finish my paper route tonight. What do you think, Yap? Enough adventure for one night?"

"Yap!"

And they set off for home.

ABOUT THE AUTHOR

Eva Mills

Eva was born in Melbourne, Australia, in 1966, and still lives there. Whenever her schedule allows, however, she goes to the countryside to write.

In 1996, Eva took a professional writing and editing course. Several of her stories have been published in books for schoolchildren.

Eva says that *Simon and the Aliens* is based on a true story told to her by a friend who used to deliver newspapers!

What do you think?

ABOUT THE ILLUSTRATOR

Gus Gordon

Gus Gordon is a freelance cartoonist and silly picture drawer. Gus draws cartoons for a variety of magazines, teaches cartooning, and belongs to the oldest cartooning club in the world.

As a young man, Gus worked on cattle ranches. He attended Agricultural College for a while—where he found himself continually drawing silly pictures! So, he left to become a cartoonist.

Gus loves illustrating children's books. When he is not drawing, he enjoys surfing, diving, and reading books with lots of pictures.